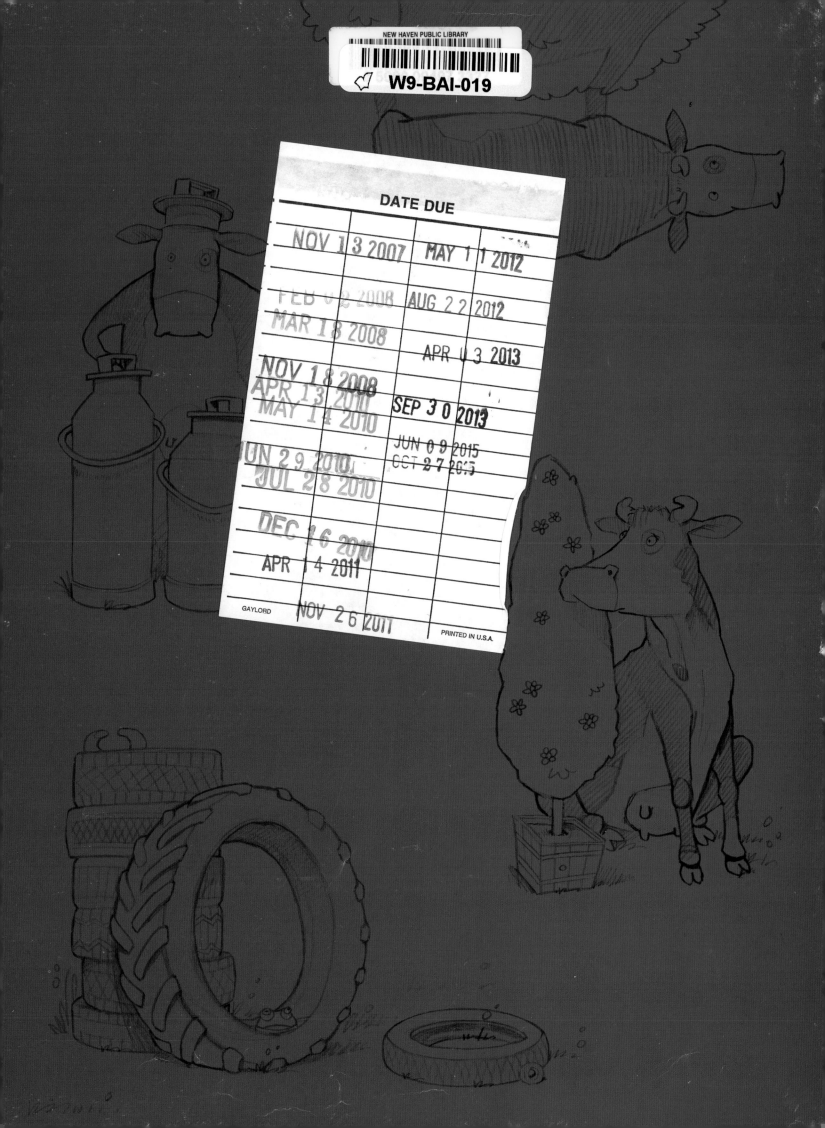

Text and Illustrations: Alexander Steffensmeier
© 2006 Patmos Verlag GmbH & Co. KG
Sauerländer Verlag, Düsseldorf
Translation copyright © 2007 by Patmos Verlag
First published as *Lieselotte Lauert* in 2006 by Patmos Verlag, Germany

Published in the United States of America in 2007 by
Walker Publishing Company, Inc.
Distributed to the trade by Holtzbrinck Publishers

For information about permission to reproduce selections from
this book, write to Permissions, Walker & Company,
104 Fifth Avenue, New York, New York 10011

Library of Congress Cataloging-in-Publication Data
Steffensmeier, Alexander.
[Lieselotte Lauert. English.]
Millie waits for the mail / Alexander Steffensmeier.
p.   cm.
Summary: Millie the cow loves to scare the mailman and chase him off the farm,
until the mailman comes up with a plan that ends up pleasing everyone.
ISBN-13: 978-0-8027-9662-2 • ISBN-10: 0-8027-9662-1 (hardcover)
ISBN-13: 978-0-8027-9663-9 • ISBN-10: 0-8027-9663-X (reinforced bdg.)
[1. Cows—Fiction. 2. Letter carriers—Fiction.] I. Title.
PZ7.S81712Mi 2007   [E]—dc22   2006035326

Visit Walker & Company's Web site at www.walkeryoungreaders.com

Printed in China
10 9 8 7 6 5 4 3 2 1

Every morning while being milked,
Millie stared out at the farmyard.

Millie
Waits
for
the
Mail

Alexander
Steffensmeier

WALKER & COMPANY
New York

This was her favorite
time of day. Because there was
something Millie loved more
than anything else—

scaring the mail carrier . . .

. . . and chasing him off the farm.

Every day
Millie searched
for a new hiding place.

On the days the farmer didn't get any mail,
Millie felt so let down.

The farmer
didn't share
Millie's idea of fun.

All her
packages

arrived broken.

Millie had to be stopped.

And the mail carrier had terrible
nightmares every night.

But one morning, he finally had
an idea.

"Maybe if I bring
the cow a package,"
he said to himself,
"she will like me."

The next day, Millie lay in wait,
just as she did every morning.

And Millie scared the mail carrier, just as she did
every morning.

"That's

enough!" shouted the farmer,

chasing after Millie,
who was chasing after
the mail carrier . . . again.

"Stop right there!"

"Enough already!"
shouted the mail carrier too.
"This package is for *you,*
you silly cow."

Millie slid to a sudden stop.
A package? She had never
received a package before.
What on earth
could it be?

The box bounced right past her
and landed under the wheels of the
farmer's tractor.

"Oh, no!" yelled the
farmer, but it was too
late.

The package was completely flattened.

Millie's heart dropped and her feet went out from under her.

And when she pulled herself up on wobbly knees, the mail carrier's bicycle looked a little different.

"I'm ruined," sniffed the mail carrier. "How will I deliver the mail without my bicycle?"

Now, every morning Millie can't wait to finish her milking. Because there is something she loves more than anything else—

delivering the mail.